Mouse & Mole

and the Year-Round Garden

Printed in the United States of America.

Scientific American Books for Young Readers is an imprint of W. H. Freeman and Company, 41 Madison Avenue, New York, NY 10010.

Library of Congress Cataloging-in-Publication Data

Cushman, Doug.
Mouse and Mole and the year-round garden / by Doug Cushman.
Summary: Two friends, Mouse and Mole, work in their garden and learn about the natural world during each season of the year.

ISBN 0-7167-6524-1
[1. Seasons—Fiction. 2. Gardening—Fiction. 3. Nature—Fiction. 4. Animals—Fiction.] I. Title.
PZ7.C959Mo 1994
[E]— dc20

93-37202
CIP
AC

10 9 8 7 6 5 4 3 2 1

For Marc Gave and Kay Kudlinski

Mouse & Mole

and the Year-Round Garden

by Doug Cushman

Radishes

Tomatoes

BOOKS FOR YOUNG READERS

Scientific American

W. H. FREEMAN AND COMPANY   NEW YORK

One day in early spring, Mole was in his tool shed
when Mouse stopped by for a visit.

"What are you looking at?" Mouse asked.

"I'm looking at my seeds and baby plants," said Mole.
"They just arrived. I'm going to begin planting my
vegetable garden today. Do you want to help?"

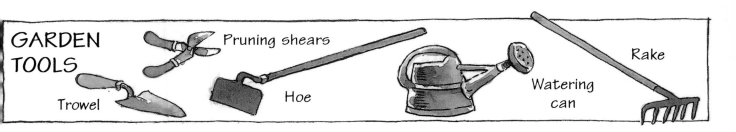

GARDEN
TOOLS

Pruning shears

Trowel

Hoe

Watering
can

Rake

Mole showed Mouse how to plant pea seeds. Then Mole planted the baby broccoli plants.

"When will the peas come up?" asked Mouse.

"Not for a while," Mole said. "We have to wait for the sun and the rain to make them grow."

"Oh," said Mouse. "I hate waiting. What can we do while we wait?"

HOW A SEED GROWS

Pea

"When it rains, we can splash in the puddles,"
said Mole.

| WHAT IS RAIN? | Water evaporates from oceans, lakes, and rivers. | It makes a cloud.  | When the cloud gets too heavy...  it rains! |

"And we can watch the water rushing under
the bridge."

A PLANT NEEDS WATER

The roots take in water.

Tubes in the stems carry it to the leaves.

"After the rain we might see a rainbow!" said Mouse.
And they did.

TO MAKE A RAINBOW

Sunlight

A prism (made of glass) breaks up sunlight into different colors.

Water drops act like prisms.

Peas

Broccoli

A few weeks later Mole said, "See how the rain and sun have made the garden grow?"

"The peas have flowers," said Mouse.

FLOWERS

Pollen

Petal

Stem — Leaf

Nectar inside

Bees visit flowers and get nectar to make honey.

Pollen on legs

At the same time they carry pollen to other flowers.

Spring turned into summer. The days were warm and sunny. The plants in Mole's garden grew tall. He planted new ones.

"The corn and the peppers are still small," said Mouse. "What shall we do while we wait for them to grow?"

Peas

Broccoli

Tomatoes

PHOTOSYNTHESIS

A leaf gets energy from sunlight... and carbon dioxide gas from the air... and makes food for the plant. The leaf gives off oxygen gas.

Peppers

Corn

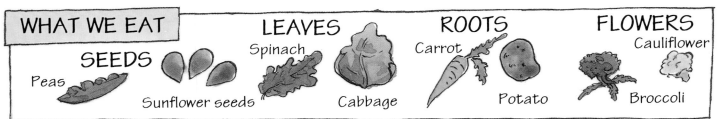

WHAT WE EAT

SEEDS

Peas

Sunflower seeds

LEAVES

Spinach

Cabbage

ROOTS

Carrot

Potato

FLOWERS

Cauliflower

Broccoli

"We can go to the beach," said Mole.
"We can swim and play in the sand.

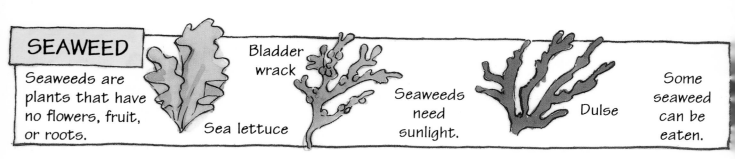

SEAWEED

Seaweeds are plants that have no flowers, fruit, or roots.

Sea lettuce

Bladder wrack

Seaweeds need sunlight.

Dulse

Some seaweed can be eaten.

"Then we can go camping in the woods and
sit around a campfire watching fireflies."

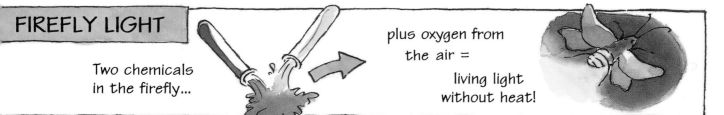

FIREFLY LIGHT

Two chemicals
in the firefly...

plus oxygen from
the air =

living light
without heat!

Soon there was much to do in the garden.
"The corn and peppers are ready to eat,"
said Mole, "and so are the tomatoes."
"But there are so many of them!" said Mouse.
"Don't worry," said Mole. "We will can the
tomatoes and make corn relish for the winter."

Peas

Broccoli

Tomatoes

UNDER
THE
GARDEN

Earthworm

Ants

Grub
(baby beetle)

Aphid

Peppers

Corn

"The garden is all done," said Mouse. "There is no more work to do."

"There is one more job," said Mole. "We must get the garden ready for next spring. We will turn the soil over and feed it."

COMPOST, FOOD FOR THE SOIL

Recycle banana peels, leaves, tomatoes, grass clippings, and weeds...

Worms and bugs eat it all.

As it decays, it becomes rich, new soil.

"Then we can go hiking up a mountain trail while
the weather is cool," said Mole.

LIFE OF A BUTTERFLY

Caterpillar
hatches from egg...

becomes
a pupa
inside a
chrysalis...

and leaves
as an adult.

"And we can watch the trees turn bright colors.

CHANGING COLORS

The chemical chlorophyll makes leaves green. In the fall leaves stop making chlorophyll...

and other colors show.

"Then we can rake a big pile of leaves in the front yard and jump into them!"

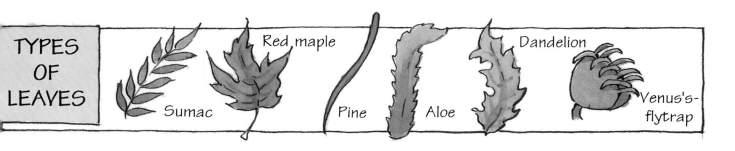

TYPES OF LEAVES

Sumac

Red maple

Pine

Aloe

Dandelion

Venus's-flytrap

"The apples are ready to pick now," said Mole.
"Yum!" said Mouse.

FRUIT FROM A FLOWER

Sepals underneath

After an apple blossom has been pollinated...

Sepals

it grows into an apple!

Dried sepals

"Look!" said Mole. "The birds are flying south.
That means winter is not far away."

When winter arrived, there was no more work to do in the garden. But Mouse and Mole could still have fun. "Let's make a snow mouse," said Mole.
And they did.

SNOW!

Tiny specs of dust and water are in clouds.

0°C 32°F

When the air is freezing...

ice forms around the dust...

and snow falls.

No two snowflakes are alike.

| MANY
PLANTS
"SLEEP"
IN WINTER | Some trees lose their leaves...  but are still alive. | Many seeds "sleep" or "rest" underground. 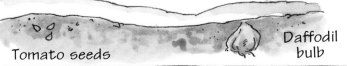 Tomato seeds   Daffodil bulb |

"Let's go sledding on the hill," said Mole.
"Not so fast!" shouted Mouse.

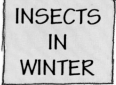

INSECTS
IN
WINTER

Some butterflies fly south.

Cricket eggs
stay buried
underground.

Some insects
sleep underground.

Ladybug

Wasps sleep
in tree bark.

"We can make some snow angels," said Mouse.

"And go skating on the pond."
And they did.

WINTER
AT THE
POND

ICE

Spotted turtle

Bass

Sunfish

Frog

Water snake

When it was too cold to stay outside, Mouse and Mole
went indoors for some hot chocolate.

"How about some spaghetti and tomato sauce with
fresh canned tomatoes and peppers from the garden?"
asked Mole.

"Yum!" said Mouse.

FOOD FOR THE WINTER

From a summer garden...

Canning

Fruit preserves

Drying herbs

Root cellar

Carrots   Potatoes

The snow disappeared and warm breezes began to blow. Winter was almost over.

One day Mouse ran over to Mole's house.

"Mole!" he called. "Look what I got in the mail!"

"What is it?" Mole asked.

WINTER

Ready... Set...

SPRING

Grow!

"A new seed catalog," Mouse said. "We can plan
our garden for this year."
And they did.